D0647002

SACRAMENTO PUBLIC LIBRARY
828 "I" Street
Sacramento, CA 95814
4/10

written by Harriet Ziefert

Clara Ann Cookie

illustrated by Emily Bolam

HOUGHTON MIFFLIN COMPANY 1999

Walter Lorraine Books

For Fred Ehrlich

Walter Lorraine Books

Text copyright © 1999 by Harriet Ziefert
Illustrations copyright © 1999 by Emily Bolam

All rights reserved. For information about permission to reproduce selections from this book, write to Permissions, Houghton Mifflin Company, 215 Park Avenue South, New York, New York 10003.

Library of Congress Cataloging-in-Publication Data

Ziefert, Harriet.
Clara Ann Cookie / written by Harriet Ziefert : illustrated by Emily Bolam.
p. cm.
Summary: When Clara does not want to get dressed, her mother encourages her to make the meanest, ugliest, scariest faces in the mirror while she assists the girl in putting on her clothes.
ISBN 0-395-92324-7
(1. Clothing and dress—Fiction. 2. Stories in rhyme.)
I. Bolam, Emily, ill. II. Title.
PZ78.3.747C1 1999
[E]—dc21 98-36603
CIP
AC

Printed in China for Harriet Ziefert, Inc.
HZI 10 9 8 7 6 5 4 3 2 1

When Clara Ann Cookie
Had to get dressed,
She got grumpy and grouchy
And very distressed.

Mother said, "Will!"
Clara said, "Won't!"
Mother said, "Do!"
Clara said, "Don't!"

Poor Clara Ann Cookie
Started to cry,
'Til her mother said, "Clara,
Here's something to try."

"A face-making game
In which you let me see
Just how angry and stubborn
You can possibly be."

"Try," said her mother,
"To look very mean—
Like the worst little girl
Whom I've ever seen."

"Good!" said her mother.
"Now look very mad.
People will say,
Oh, that girl is so bad!"

"Now make a scary face,
As if you had seen
Us all being eaten
By a monster machine."

"Good!" said her mother.
"Now darling, please make
A face that's so ugly
The mirror will break."

"Look sick!" said her mother.
"And sit on your bed.
I'll get a cool washcloth
To put on your head."

"Good!" said her mother.
"Now be snooty, as if I'd said,
I wish stuck-up Clara
Would fall on her head!"

"Now happy and silly
As a small girl can be,
You can dance and giggle
And yell, *Look at me!*"

"Let's see Clara's face,
So pretty and sweet.

Surprise! She's all dressed
From her head...

to her feet.